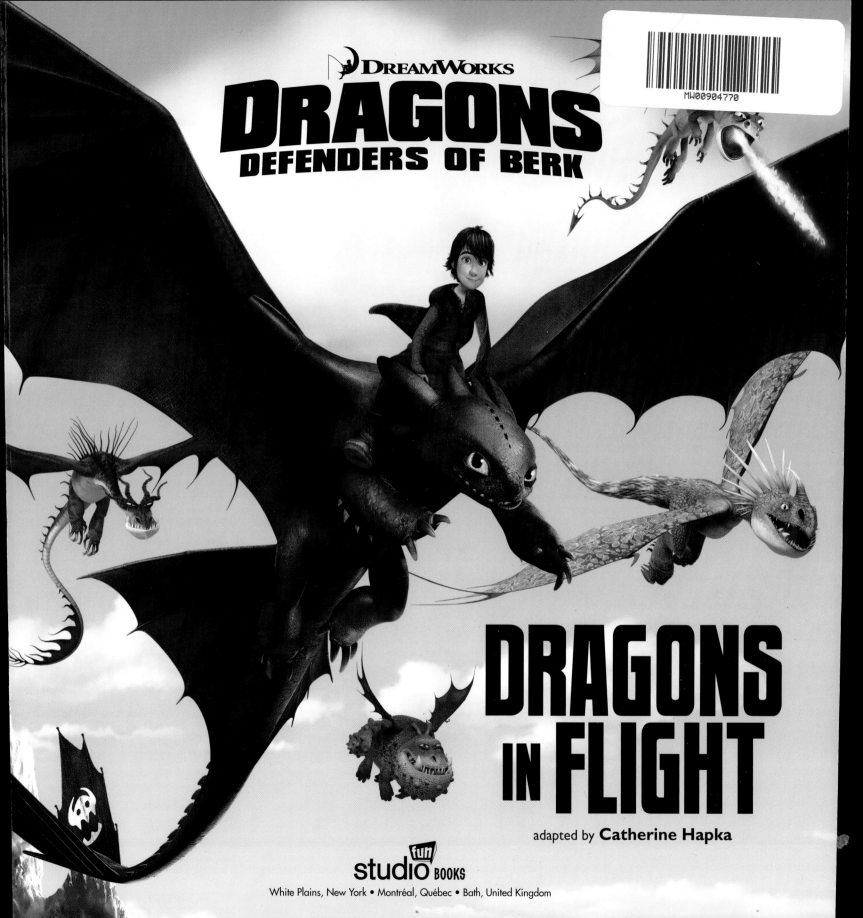

DREAMWORKS
DRAGONS
DEFENDERS OF BERK

DRAGONS IN FLIGHT

adapted by **Catherine Hapka**

studio fun **BOOKS**

White Plains, New York • Montréal, Québec • Bath, United Kingdom

Now that the dragons are living in our village, my dad, Stoick, has started a Dragon Training Academy. And guess who's the head dragon trainer? Yours truly—that would be me, Hiccup.

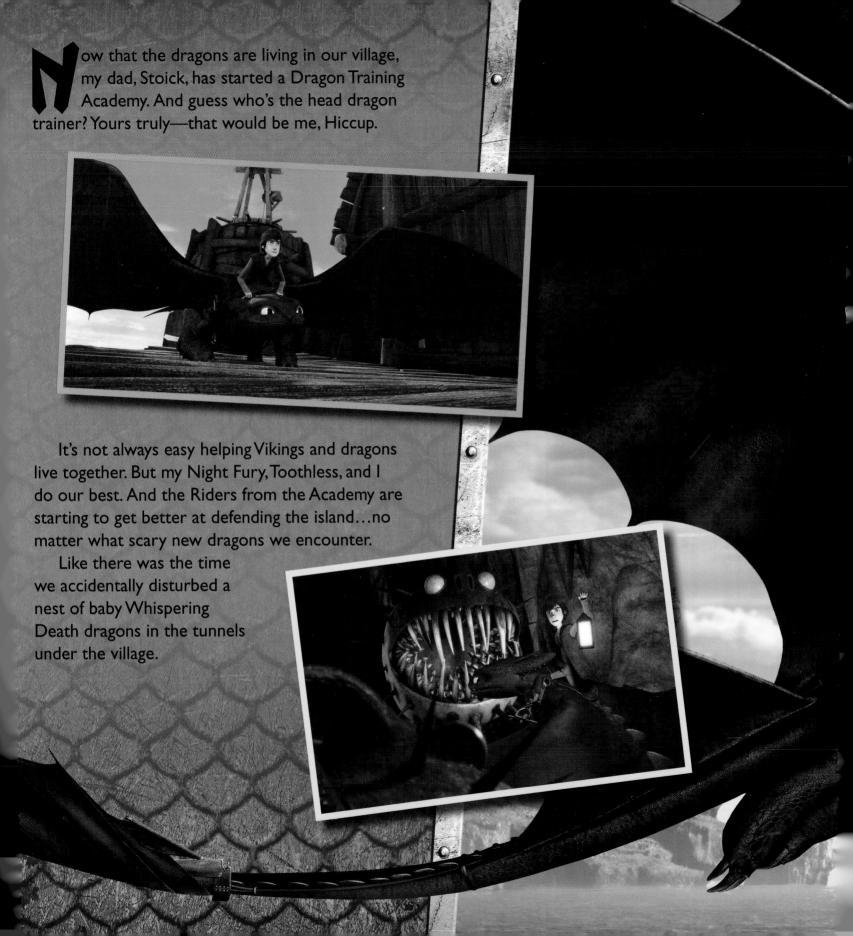

It's not always easy helping Vikings and dragons live together. But my Night Fury, Toothless, and I do our best. And the Riders from the Academy are starting to get better at defending the island…no matter what scary new dragons we encounter.

Like there was the time we accidentally disturbed a nest of baby Whispering Death dragons in the tunnels under the village.

That was scary enough, but it wasn't the worst part, though. The worst part? The nest's leader was a super powerful, super rare dragon called the Screaming Death. He's so rare he wasn't even part of Fishlegs' Dragon cards!

The Screaming Death was tough to beat. But the Dragon Riders passed the test—we drove the dangerous wild dragons away from Berk. For now, at least…

Things sure are never boring at the Academy! One of the more exciting days was when Snotlout and Fishlegs started arguing about who was a better dragon trainer. That led to a crazy competition to see who could do the best job training a Terrible Terror. Terrible Terrors may be small and cute, but like their name suggests, they have terrible tempers!

I thought the whole competition was a bad idea. But what do you know? The training really paid off!

Alvin the Treacherous kidnapped Meatlug! When we went to rescue her, Alvin threatened to put his sword through Meatlug.

This is where our Terrible Terror training came in handy. Astrid had taught her Terrible Terror to sneak up on people. She sent it down to distract Alvin. Meanwhile, Fishlegs sent his Terror to steal Alvin's sword, while mine freed Meatlug. Finally the twins' Terrible Terrors helped Meatlug free herself.

So Meatlug was saved, and we were a team again! Who knew Terrible Terrors—or a little competition—could be so useful?

Ruffnut and Tuffnut have never been the best students at the Academy. So it wasn't a huge surprise when one day they got themselves in trouble by springing an old dragon trap. Tuffnut ended up in the trap, and Ruffnut had to go for help. Ruffnut can't fly their two-headed Hideous Zippleback, Barf & Belch, on her own, so she left the dragon protecting Tuffnut and hiked back to town.

There was just one problem…well, one MORE problem. It was dry season, and when Barf & Belch were attacked by a Typhoomerang, their fireball sparked a huge blaze that threatened the whole island!

When Toothless and I arrived, I recognized the Typhoomerang. It was Torch! I hadn't seen him since he was a baby. Luckily he wasn't a baby anymore, and he flew us all to safety.

Then the twins surprised everyone by coming up with a way to save the village by fighting fire with fire—literally. All the dragons helped, and Berk was safe again. Well, at least until the next time the twins get themselves into trouble…

Everyone in Berk was amazed when one day we found a Skrill trapped in a chunk of ice. The Skrill is a legendary dragon, and an extra scary one. It can harness the power of lightning!

Dagur the Deranged, one of our biggest enemies, found out about the frozen Skrill and came after it. Unfortunately for all of us, someone else got there first—our OTHER biggest enemy, Alvin the Treacherous!

Before we knew it, our two greatest enemies were working together. Well, sort of. They couldn't seem to decide who would get to control the Skrill. Could their bickering be our chance to sneak in, free the Skrill, and defeat both tribes? I wasn't sure, but I knew we had to try…

The twins and I flew to Alvin's camp. But the Skrill was already gone!

It turned out Dagur broke his deal with Alvin and snatched the dragon. With the power of the Skrill, Dagur would be unbeatable! We had to free the huge dragon—or else.

Luckily, Dagur hates me and Toothless so much that he let the Skrill loose— to attack us. We almost got struck by lightning so many times I lost count.

Then I saw a crevice in the glacier and had an idea. I aimed Toothless into the crevice, and the Skrill followed. We led it on a wild chase, until finally I saw my chance.

CRASH! Thinking our reflection was really us, the Skrill knocked himself out on the ice. Barf & Belch finished the job by blasting the crevice shut. Soon the Skrill was trapped deep in the ice once again.

We can only hope Dagur never finds it there.

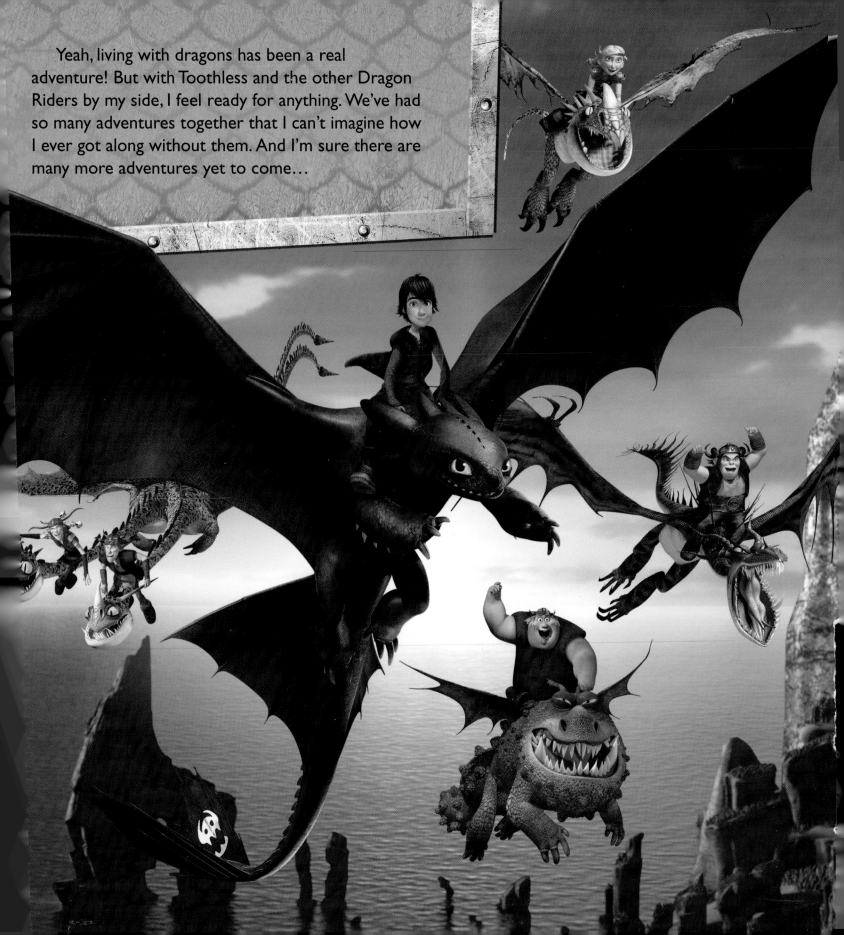

Yeah, living with dragons has been a real adventure! But with Toothless and the other Dragon Riders by my side, I feel ready for anything. We've had so many adventures together that I can't imagine how I ever got along without them. And I'm sure there are many more adventures yet to come...